Billie's GREAT DESERT ADVENTURE

by Sally Rippin

illustrated by Alisa Coburn

Kane Miller
A DIVISION OF EDC PUBLISHING

Billie B. Brown SKIPS into preschool.

"Bye, Daddy!" calls Billie.

She is excited to
be at preschool today.

"Can we go outside and play?" asks Billie.
"Look! I have my duck boots on."

"No, Billie," says Miss Amy.
"It's too wet to play outside
today."

"A rainy day is a good day for reading,"
says Miss Amy, leading Billie into the classroom.

Billie frowns.

She doesn't want
to read. She wants to
stomp in puddles.

What's the point of having puddle-stomping duck boots if no one will let you stomp in puddles?

Billie flops onto the cushions.

When her friend Jack comes over,
Billie pulls the cushions over her
head so he can't see her.

She feels too cross to play
with anyone right now.

Even Jack.

Jack lifts a cushion.

COOL!
A cave!
he says.

Jack's right. It does
look like a cave!

Jack squeezes through
the hole into the
deep dark cave.

Billie wriggles
through, too.

Inside the cave it
is gloomy and a
little bit spooky.

They have found a treasure
chamber! Billie and Jack
wrap each other in jewels
and precious things that
gleam and glitter like stars.

Suddenly, a deep voice calls out.

A big stone wall rolls back, and there stand forty thieves with swords in their hands and fury in their faces.

RUN!

yells Billie.

Billie grabs Jack's hand
and they slip past
the angry thieves …

… to where their
magic carpet is
waiting for them.

Billie and Jack jump
onto the magic carpet.

The carpet climbs into the sky,
racing over the hot shimmering desert.

up

up

up

Faster and faster they fly,
but the furious thieves are
close behind them.

Oh no! The carpet is getting tired carrying its heavy load. The thieves are catching up!

splutter

cough

groan

The thieves reach out and grab at the carpet.

Billie and Jack are trapped!
  The thieves close in around them.

Just then, Billie has an idea.

A **Super-duper** idea.

Throw the treasure! she shouts.

The thieves **Scramble** and *wriggle*
and *wrestle* in the sand for the jewels.

The thieves are so busy rolling around that they
don't even notice Billie and Jack flying away.

Quick as two sticks, Billie and Jack fly back to the cave. But a huge stone is blocking the cave's entrance.

"Oh no!" groans Billie.
"What's the secret password?"

Open Sesame! *he shouts.*

Jack smiles.

And the big stone rumbles back to reveal the cave.

Slowly, slowly, Billie and Jack inch back along the dark scary passages …

… and pop up
out of the cave.

Just in time
for fruit snack.